# Little Men

Retold from the Louisa May Alcott
original by Deanna McFadden

Illustrated by Dan Andreasen

STERLING

New York / London
www.sterlingpublishing.com/kids

STERLING and the distinctive Sterling logo
are registered trademarks of Sterling Publishing Co., Inc.

**Library of Congress Cataloging-in-Publication Data**

McFadden, Deanna.
 Little men / retold from the Louisa May Alcott original ; abridged by Deanna
McFadden ; illustrated by Dan Andreasen ; afterword by Arthur Pober.
   p. cm.
 Summary: An abridged version of the Louisa May Alcott novel that follows the
adventures of Jo March and her husband Professor Bhaer as they try to make their
school for boys a happy, comfortable, and stimulating place.
 ISBN-13: 978-1-4027-5423-4
 ISBN-10: 1-4027-5423-X
 [1. Boarding schools—Fiction. 2. Schools—Fiction. 3. Family life—New
England—Fiction. 4. New England—History—19th century—Fiction.] I.
Andreasen, Dan, ill. II. Alcott, Louisa May, 1832–1888. Little men. III. Title.
PZ7.M4784548Lh 2009
[Fic]—dc22
                                                                        2008003165
                                    Lot#:
                              4  6  8  10  9  7  5
                                    11/17

                      Published by Sterling Publishing Co., Inc.
                       387 Park Avenue South, New York, NY 10016
                        Text copyright © 2009 by Deanna McFadden
                       Illustrations copyright © 2009 by Dan Andreasen
                         Distributed in Canada by Sterling Publishing
                    $^{c}/_{o}$ Canadian Manda Group, 165 Dufferin Street,
                             Toronto, Ontario, Canada M6K 3H6
               Distributed in the United Kingdom by GMC Distribution Services,
                 Castle Place, 166 High Street, Lewes, East Sussex, England BN7 1XU
                   Distributed in Australia by Capricorn Link (Australia) Pty. Ltd.
                         P.O. Box 704, Windsor, NSW 2756, Australia

                 Classic Starts is a trademark of Sterling Publishing Co., Inc.

                                 *Printed in China*
                                *All rights reserved*

                      Sterling ISBN 978-1-4027-5423-4

            For information about custom editions, special sales, premium and
                   corporate purchases, please contact Sterling Special Sales
            Department at 800-805-5489 or specialsales@sterlingpublishing.com.

# Contents

∽

# CHAPTER 1

## Nat Comes to Plumfield

The ragged boy looked up at the gate in front of him and stammered, "Pl . . . please, sir, is this Plumfield?" Nat Blake didn't know if he was in the right place.

"Yes," the old man at the gate answered. "This is Plumfield. Who sent you?"

"Mr. Laurence gave me a letter for Mrs. Jo Bhaer, the lady of the house."

The old man opened the gate and said, "In that case, I'm sure she's expecting you. Go on up."

The man's kind words gave Nat the courage to

walk up the path to the house. Through the rain, he could see green grass, big trees, and a lovely garden. When he lifted his head, Nat saw a very large, square house with a big, old-fashioned porch.

*Goodness,* Nat thought to himself, *this would be a wonderful place to live.*

Warm light glowed from each of the windows, and Nat could hear the pleasant hum of many voices.

*I hope the lady will see me,* he thought as he knocked on the door.

A rosy-faced maid swung the door open and smiled. She wasn't at all surprised to see him. "You're wet!" she said, pointing to a bench in the hall. "Go and sit down there for a spell to dry off while I take your note to the missus."

The house swarmed with boys of all sizes who were playing a variety of indoor games as the rain fell. Nat looked around. To his right, he saw two large school rooms filled with blackboards, desks, and books. In the large room in front of him, a group of boys lay about talking in front of the fire while an older fellow beside them practiced the flute.

A large dinner table occupied the room to Nat's left. On top of it were pitchers of milk, piles of brown and white bread, and perfect stacks of gingerbread cookies. He could smell toast and baked apples as well, which made his stomach grumble.

But it was the hall that truly caught his attention. From his bench, Nat could see a gang of happy boys playing tag. On one landing of the stairs, a hearty game of marbles was going on. On the other, there was a game of checkers. The stairs held a number of fascinating things for a little boy: a kitten, two puppies, a boy reading a book, and a girl singing a lullaby to a pretty doll. Nat watched as a constant stream of boys slid down the banister. It didn't seem to matter if it

ruined their clothes or broke their limbs.

One particularly lively boy came barreling down so quickly that he could not stop and crashed to the floor. Nat ran over to the boy, who must have had a head as hard as a cannonball to survive the fall.

Expecting to find him half-dead, Nat was surprised to see the boy wink at him, and then say with a great grin, "Hello!"

"Are you all right?!" Nat asked.

"Oh, just fine!" the boy replied. "Are you new? What's your name? How old are you?"

"I don't know if I'm to stay yet, but my name is Nat Blake and I'm twelve." Nat answered.

The boy jumped up off the floor and said, "Well, thunder turtles, I'm glad we're the same age. I'm Tommy Bangs. Why don't you come up and have a go? I'm sure Mother Jo won't mind."

Nat lowered his head. "I think I should wait here until I find out whether I'm to stay or not."

"Say, Demi," Tommy called out, "here's a new fellow! Come down and keep him company while he waits to talk to Mother Jo."

The boy reading on the stairs looked up from his book, then came down to see Nat and asked, "Did Uncle Laurie send you?"

Nat nodded. "Is that Mr. Laurence?"

"He's my uncle," Demi said, "and he always sends nice boys."

Nat smiled, and the two stood there awkwardly for a moment until the little girl with the doll came to join them.

"This is my twin sister, Daisy," Demi said.

Nat thought they looked very much alike, as twins should, even if they were brother and sister. She nodded at Nat, who smiled back.

"I do hope you get to stay," Daisy said. "We have such good times here, don't we, Demi?"

"Of course we do," her brother replied. "That's why Aunt Jo *has* Plumfield."

"It seems a very nice place indeed," Nat said.

"Oh, it's the nicest place in the world, isn't it, Demi?" Daisy said.

"No," Demi answered carefully. "I think Greenland, where the icebergs and seals live, is nicer. But that doesn't mean I'm not fond of Plumfield. I mean, it is a *very* nice place to be."

Demi had just been reading a book on Greenland. He was about to open up the book so he could show Nat the pictures when the maid came back to tell the boy he could stay.

"I'm so glad," Daisy said. "Let's go see Aunt

Jo." She took Nat by the hand, which made him feel right at home. Demi returned to his book as his sister led the new boy into the back room. Inside, a stout gentleman wrestled with two little boys on the sofa while a thin lady read Nat's letter.

"Aunty, he's here!" Daisy called. "Nat, this is Aunt Jo."

"So," Jo replied, "you are Nat, my new boy! It's lovely to see you. I know you'll be happy here."

She drew Nat to her and stroked his hair in a very motherly way. She had a merry face, and although she wasn't entirely handsome, her whole person was jolly as she said, "I am Mother Jo, and that gentleman is Father Bhaer. The two boys are Rob and Teddy, our little Bhaers. Boys, come now and meet Nat."

The three wrestlers obeyed quickly and came to welcome Nat.

"There's a room of your own all ready for

you, son." Father Bhaer said. "Sit down by the fire and dry those wet shoes."

"Wet?" Mother Jo said. "Oh, so they are! Off with them this minute, and we'll have some dry things ready for you in no time."

Jo bustled around him and soon Nat was snuggled in a cozy little chair with dry socks and warm slippers on his feet.

"Thank you, ma'am," he said.

Jo smiled warmly at Nat and said with a twinkle in her eye, "Those slippers belong to Tommy Bangs, but he never remembers to put them on when he's in the house, so you'll have them instead."

Nat coughed loudly.

"We're going to need to keep you very warm if we're to heal that cough," Jo said. "How long have you had it?"

"All winter. It just won't get better."

Jo sighed. "No wonder, with you living in a

damp cellar with hardly a rag on your poor back." She looked over to her husband, who seemed to know exactly what she was thinking.

"Rob, why don't you go ask the maid to give you the cough medicine," Father Bhaer said.

Nat looked a little scared when he heard the word *medicine,* but at that very second, little Teddy started to cough as hard as he could. His face turned red and his eyes practically bulged out of his head.

"Look at that silly Teddy," Jo said. "He's trying to make himself cough because the medicine has honey in it, and he does love the taste."

After he had his dose of medicine, Nat rested in the cozy chair by the fire. He had barely closed his eyes when a large bell sounded. It was time for dinner.

CHAPTER 2

# Nat's First Night

༄

When Nat went into the dining room, he saw twelve boys, six on each side of the table, standing behind their proper chairs. They fidgeted, but no one sat down until Mother Jo had taken her place. Teddy sat on her left, and Nat sat on her right.

"This is our new boy, Nat Blake. After supper you can say 'how do you do,' but for now let's sit down and eat."

The food was delicious, and Nat ate so much he thought he might burst. Tommy Bangs sat beside him. Nat summoned up all his courage and asked, "Who's that boy down there at the other end? He was talking to me earlier, but I can't remember his name."

"Why, that's Demi Brooke. He's Mother Jo's nephew."

"That's a funny name," Nat said.

"His real name is John, but they call him Demi-John because his father's John, too. It's a joke, you see?"

Only Nat didn't quite see, so he smiled politely and said, "He was very nice to me."

"You bet he was. And he's real smart, too. He reads a lot and knows everything."

"Who is the fellow beside him?"

"His name is Franz," Tommy answered. "He's Father Bhaer's nephew. He sees to us and teaches some."

Nat looked over at Franz. "I saw him playing the flute, didn't I?" he asked.

Tommy nodded, unable to answer because he had just stuffed an entire baked apple into his mouth. He quickly swallowed and said, "Oh, don't he play well, though? I like a good drum myself, and I'm going to learn as soon as I can."

"I can play the fiddle," Nat said.

"You can?" Tommy half-shouted. "Father Bhaer's got an old fiddle, and I just know he'd let you play it."

Nat smiled. "Really? I think I would like that very much. I used to go around fiddling with my father for money until he died."

"Wasn't that fun?" Tommy cried with excitement.

"No, it was awful. We were always outside, winter or summer. When I got tired, my father got angry. And we never had enough to eat," Nat said. "But I do miss my little fiddle."

Before turning back to his supper, Tommy said, "Well, we've got a jolly band here that you can play with if you're any good. Just wait until tomorrow night. You'll see!"

Jo looked at the new boy and smiled to herself. Laurie was right—he was the perfect kind of boy for Plumfield. Despite his illness, his blue eyes sparkled, and she was sure his pale, thin frame would soon be improved with good meals and kindness.

After dinner, Jo had a word with Father Bhaer, who took his old fiddle out of its case. Jo came into the schoolroom where the boys were once again playing and found Nat watching them from the corner.

She walked over to the boy and said, "Here you go, Nat. It's Father Bhaer's, but he's happy to let you use it. We must have a fiddle in our Plumfield band, and we think you're just the boy to play it."

Nat took the fiddle from her at once and handled it with such care that it was plain to see how much he loved the instrument. He said, "I'll do the very best I can."

He drew the bow across the strings and played quietly as the boys started to gather around him. As Nat played louder and louder, more people stopped to listen. His cheeks flushed and his fingers flew. When he finished, they all gave him a hearty round of applause.

"You do play first-rate!" Tommy said.

"Of course you must play with us in the band!" Franz added.

Nat smiled.

Father Bhaer said, "Why don't you come over here, by the piano, and let's have some songs we can all sing?"

It was the proudest moment of Nat's life as he was lead to the place of honor by the piano beside the other musicians, who gathered their instruments. After a few false starts, they all got going: flute, piano, and fiddle. Nat tapped his foot in time and played with a great smile on his face. It was so different to be in a lovely warm room surrounded by people who were all smiling. He wasn't out in the cold. He wasn't playing for pennies. But then the excitement became a bit too much for little Nat, who turned to face the corner and started to cry.

"Whatever is wrong?" Jo asked.

Nat answered, "You've all been so kind to me. I just can't help it." And then he started coughing until he had no breath left.

"Come with me, my dear. You need to rest. You are worn out on your first night here."

Jo led the boy back into her parlor, where she cuddled with him until he told her all of his troubles. "This is your home now," she replied when he had finished. "All you need to do is get well and strong so you can take part in as much music as your heart wishes."

Then she took him upstairs to see Asia, the

maid, who gave Nat a bath and cut his hair. Before Jo tucked him into bed, she gave him another dose of medicine. The warm, dry room felt like heaven.

Just as he was about to fall asleep, a pillow fight broke out down the hall. Nat sat up and looked around for Jo.

She laughed. "We always allow one pillow fight on Saturday night! We change the pillowcases tomorrow, and it puts the glow back in the boys' faces before bed."

"This is such a nice school!" Nat said.

"It's an odd one," Jo said, "but we don't believe in making the children miserable by having too many rules. We've got a good bargain—we allow fifteen minutes on Saturday night, and the boys promise to go to bed on time every other night without fail. So far, it's worked."

Jo rang a small bell and shouted, "Time's up, boys! Everyone get into bed!"

Tommy shouted the final battle cheer as Demi threw the very last pillow. The boys settled into their beds with barely a whisper, and soon all were asleep. After settling down the boys in the other rooms, Jo came in to kiss Nat on the head and wish him sweet dreams.

CHAPTER 3

# A Happy Sunday

~

Nat leaped out of bed the instant the bell rang the next morning. He found new clothes laid out on the chair, and he was almost dressed when Tommy came barreling into his room and said, "Let's go down for breakfast!"

Father Bhaer said a short grace, and then everyone enjoyed the Sunday morning feast of weak tea, steak, and baked potatoes—much more than their usual toast and butter. A walk was planned, and the Sunday lessons were laid out. Nat thought that it would be a wonderful day, for he did love the idea of a quiet peaceful Sunday, even if he had never truly had one.

"Now, boys," Father Bhaer said, "run and get your chores done so you can all be ready when the omnibus comes to take us to church."

With breakfast finished, everyone set to their tasks. Soon, the older boys were ready and waiting for the bus. Nat still had a bad cough, so he stayed home with the younger boys, who learned their Sunday lessons with Jo in her parlor.

"Nat," Jo called, "come and see here." She showed him a closet filled with picture books, paint boxes, building blocks, little diaries, and materials for writing letters.

"This is my Sunday closet," she said to him. "I want my boys to love Sunday, to find it a peaceful, pleasant day—a time to rest and learn the lessons meant for that day." Jo opened a large book and showed it to Nat.

"Why, that's my name!" he said.

"Yes, I have a page for each boy. I keep a little account of how he gets on through the week and show it to him on Sunday. It's the way I help each of them to be better boys. It's my Conscience Book. No one sees it but me and the boy whose name is at the top of the page."

In his whole life, Nat had never met anyone like Mother Jo. While he was thinking this very thought, she tweaked his ear and said, "Why don't you practice the hymns for tonight?"

Alone with his beloved fiddle and a new music book, Nat enjoyed an hour or two of genuine happiness before Father Bhaer and the boys returned from church.

After lunch, Father Bhaer and many of the boys set out for a walk. Because he was sick, Nat stayed back. Tommy stayed with him. The pair went for a short stroll around Plumfield so Tommy could show him the land.

The long driveway around the house led to an

old corn barn. Inside were animals of all shapes and sizes: guinea pigs, mice, birds, a donkey, dogs, and hens.

"My father sent me the money for the hens once he heard we were to raise them ourselves," Tommy explained, and pointed to a sign that identified the hens as his. "That's how most of the boys got their pets. People either gave 'em to us or we bought them with money from our parents."

Nat nodded, sad because he had no parents to send him money for a pet.

"Mother Jo lets me sell the eggs to her, and a little bit goes back to my father each time to pay him back. Oh, I always give her a fair price," Tommy said. "I'd be ashamed not to."

Nat looked around at all the animals and said, "They are all great pets, but I think if I should have one, I would like the donkey."

Tommy nodded. "Mr. Laurie sent Toby over

so Mother Jo wouldn't have to carry Teddy on our walks. He is a very good little donkey."

Nat looked around the barn as Tommy collected the eggs from his hens.

"I wish I had a dove, a turtle, or even a hen to call my own," Nat said.

Tommy thought hard for a minute. "Look here," he said. "This is what we'll do. If you will hunt eggs with me, I'll give you one egg out of every dozen. Once you've collected twelve, Mother Jo will give you twenty-five cents and you can buy anything you'd like."

"I'll do it!" Nat shouted, "You are a kind fellow, Tommy."

"It's no bother. Start down here. I heard Granny crackling, so I know she's laid some eggs somewhere."

The boys managed to find two more eggs, which Tommy added to his last dozen. Before they left the barn, Tommy changed his sign so it read: T. BANGS & Co. Now everyone would know he now had a partner in the egg-finding business.

Back outside, Tommy led Nat to an old willow tree. They scrambled up onto a wide branch with two little seats attached to it.

"This is Demi's and my private place," Tommy said. "No one except Daisy can come unless we let him."

Down below, Nat could see the brook bubbling. Above him, the leaves rustled. "I hope you'll let me come up sometimes, too," he said.

"As long as it's okay with Demi, but I don't think he'll mind. Last night he told me he liked you."

"He did?" Nat asked.

"Sure," Tommy replied. "Demi likes quiet chaps. You two will get along okay if you like books as much as he does."

Nat grew very quiet and said, "I don't know

how to read much. I was always playing the fiddle."

"Twelve years old and can't read!" Tommy shook his head. He pulled a book out from a shelf in the hollow of the tree and handed it to Nat. Then he helped Nat with his reading for most of the afternoon.

Between chapters, Tommy told Nat all about the garden and the little patches of farm that belonged to each boy. "We can raise what we like in it, only we each have to choose different things and tend to them all summer."

"What did you choose?" Nat asked.

"Beans," Tommy replied, "because they're easier than corn or potatoes. I tried melons last year, and what a disaster. The bugs were a bother, and the old things just wouldn't ripen. At the end of the summer, I was left with one poor watermelon and a bunch of old mushy melons."

Nat laughed and said, "Corn looks pretty as it grows."

"Yes," Tommy said, "but you have to hoe it over and over again. Six weeks' beans, well, they only have to be hoed once or so, and they ripen so quickly."

"I wonder if I'll have a garden."

"Of course you will!" a voice called up from below.

It was Father Bhaer, who had come to find them. He tried to have a nice chat with every boy each Sunday. Nat climbed down, and he and Father Bhaer set off to explore the garden plots. They found a little corner for Nat to call his own, and Father Bhaer explained how important it was to keep up with the crops. It was the food they would depend on for much of the year.

Back at Plumfield, all the boys were getting ready for dinner. The Sunday meal was a jolly occasion, and soon everyone was back in Jo's parlor to hear Father Bhaer tell a story. As he looked around, Nat thought the boys seemed more like a great family than a group of school children.

Father Bhaer began. He told the boys a fable about a magical garden and thirteen little gardeners who each had to work hard to keep their vegetables growing. Some gardeners flourished, while others learned that if one lets them, weeds can grow even in the best of soils.

"Why," Demi cried, "I think he means us! We're the soil, and if we let the weeds grow inside us, we'll never sprout properly."

Everyone laughed, but Father Bhaer said that Demi was correct. Then Father Bhaer asked who would like to say what they would grow in their imaginary garden.

"I shall go first," Jo spoke up, "as I'm the eldest. Even if I am mother to all of you, I should think that I still need to grow some patience in my garden. Hopefully, it will fare better than Tommy's melons."

A great chuckle came at Tommy's expense. He went next and told everyone that he would try to be less forgetful. The boys all took turns, many of them wishing for the same things: patience, good tempers, and generosity.

Once the talk of the gardens finished, it was time for some music. Nat's fiddle fit right in with Franz's flute and Father Bhaer's piano. After a merry time, with sweet voices singing songs and many toes tapping in time to the lovely music, the boys went upstairs to bed — no pillow fights tonight! Nat slipped off to his room as well, happier than he had ever been in his entire life.

# CHAPTER 4

## Nat Settles In

∽

When Nat went to class on Monday morning, he was afraid to show everyone that he was so far behind. But he needn't have worried. Father Bhaer gave him a seat in the big front window so he could turn his back on the others and say his particular lessons there, where no one could hear him or see how he made a mess of his notebook. Nat worked so hard on that first day that Father Bhaer remarked, "Don't work too hard, my boy. You will tire yourself out, and there is plenty of time."

"But I must work hard or I won't catch up!" Nat said. "The other boys know heaps, and I don't know anything."

Despair had crept in as Nat heard the boys recite their grammar, history, and geography with great ease. As Franz took the rest of the class through their multiplication tables, Father Bhaer sat down beside Nat and said, "You know a good many things that they don't know."

"I do?" Nat asked.

"Yes. For one thing, you read music, and none of the other boys can do that, can they? Best of all, you really care to learn, and that is half the battle. It might be hard at first, but you must keep trying."

"I do want to learn," Nat said after some thought. "And I will try, even though it's hard because I've never gone to school before. I just hope the other lads won't laugh at me."

Demi heard this remark and piped up, "No one shall laugh at you—I won't let them!"

Having forgotten he was in the middle of a lesson, Demi looked quite surprised when the class stopped in the middle of seven times nine to look up at him. Thinking that a lesson in helping others was more important than math, Father Bhaer explained to the class that Nat had never been to school. Right then, all of the boys promised to help him.

After this first day, Jo thought it best that Nat grow healthy before going to school full-time. She kept him busy with his garden and other chores inside until his cheeks were rosy and his thin shoulders were straighter from fresh air and tender care.

Jo and Father Bhaer encouraged all of the boys, including Nat, to take on part-time jobs. They would never be rich boys, and good honest work would prepare them for life after Plumfield. Tommy sold his eggs and Franz helped with the teaching, while other boys built objects to sell.

Nat saw all of this hard work and was eager to do his share. One day he came running to Father Bhaer and said, "May I please go into the woods and play the fiddle for some people having a picnic? I'd like to earn some money as the other boys do."

Father Bhaer answered, "Of course you may. It's an easy and pleasant way to spend an afternoon, and I'm glad you have the chance to do it."

When Nat returned to Plumfield, he had two whole dollars in his pocket. "It's so much nicer than fiddling in the street," he said. "And I get to keep all the money!"

Father Bhaer laughed and said, "As long as it doesn't interfere with your lessons, you may go and play the fiddle for the picnickers whenever you like."

"I would never let anything come between me and my lessons!" Nat said.

The summer months marched on and Nat grew stronger and smarter each day. Nothing made him prouder than digging away in his little garden, playing his fiddle, and working hard at school. Over the course of a few short months, Nat had truly found a home at Plumfield.

# CHAPTER 5

# Patty-Pans

⌒

One day Jo found Daisy sitting on the stairs, pouting. It was quite unlike her niece to be this way, so Jo asked kindly, "What's the matter, Daisy?"

"The boys won't let me play with them," she replied.

Jo put her hand on the girl's shoulder and tried very hard not to smile. "And why is that?"

"Because they're playing football. Even Demi won't let me join. He used to let me, but now the boys laugh at him. I am so tired of playing alone."

"Well, I'm about to go into town to see your mother. Why don't you come along? Maybe you'd like to stay home for a couple days?"

Daisy stood up and said, "I should like to see Mother, but I don't want to stay there. I'll come back here, or else Demi will miss me."

"You'll need to find something to do while I get ready to go. Why don't you go see Asia downstairs in the kitchen. Maybe you can help her with lunch."

Daisy nodded and flew off downstairs to help Asia with her baking.

*I'll need to find something else for her to do,* Jo thought. *I never would have imagined that it's more difficult to keep one girl occupied than it is to keep a dozen boys going.*

As she put away the last of the laundry and closed the wardrobe door, Jo had an idea. "That's it!" she said out loud. "That'll be the perfect hobby for Daisy. Now if I can just figure out a way to make it work . . ."

All the way into town, Jo teased Daisy about having a grand surprise. Daisy begged her aunt to tell her what she was planning, but Jo wouldn't budge. While Jo went and did all the shopping, Daisy stayed behind with her mother. But when her aunt returned, she still wouldn't say anything about the surprise. To make matters worse, Daisy watched as her mother and aunt had a long visit that felt like forever to a little girl dying to know a secret.

Finally, it was time to go. As her mother tied on her bonnet, she said, "Be a good girl, Daisy, and learn Aunt Jo's new game. It's very kind of her to teach you, and she'll even play with you herself—although I know she doesn't like it very much."

Aunt Jo and her mother laughed.

Something rattled in the back of the carriage on the way home, and Daisy said, "Is that it? Is that the new game?"

Jo answered, "It is indeed."

"Why, it's making a lot of noise. What is it made from?"

"Iron, tin, wood, brass, sugar, salt, coal, and a hundred other things."

"How strange!" Daisy said. "What color is it?"

"All sorts of colors," Aunt Jo replied.

Daisy asked many questions, all of which her aunt answered without ever telling her the one piece of information she wanted above all others: the name of the game.

When they got home, Daisy inspected every little bundle for a clue. Then Jo took the bundles upstairs, where Daisy heard hammering and all sorts of noise. Still, no one would tell her the secret. All of this made Daisy so excited she could barely contain herself.

When she thought she simply could not wait a moment longer, Jo told her that the secret would be revealed after her lessons the next day.

As hard as it was to sleep, Daisy found school almost impossible. The bell had barely chimed when she raced to Jo's parlor and shouted, "I've done all my lessons—please tell me what the surprise is now, please!"

"It's all ready for you," Jo said as she tucked Teddy up under her arm. "Come on upstairs."

Daisy threw open the nursery door and looked around. "I don't see anything."

"But do you hear anything?" Jo asked.

Daisy stood still until she heard a large crackle from behind a curtain drawn in front of big bay window.

"Oh!" she exclaimed as she raced forward and pulled the curtains apart. "Oh my!"

Aunt Jo and her helpers had set up a small cooking stove, which was all ready to prepare an entire meal for a whole cast of hungry dolls. One of the window panes had been replaced with tin, which sent the smoke outside in a way that was of

no danger to anyone. A tea kettle steamed away on top of the stove and seemed almost as happy as Daisy herself.

Her eyes leaped from one charming object to the next until she couldn't contain her happiness any longer. She flew into her aunt's arms and said, "Oh, Aunty, it's so splendid. I can make meals and cookies and all kinds of fun. What on earth made you think of it?"

Jo laughed and said, "You always want to help Asia in the kitchen. I told your uncle Laurie, and he promptly went out and found the very best small stove he could find."

Daisy was so excited, she couldn't speak.

Jo continued, "This way you won't dirty Asia's kitchen, and you can still learn all sorts of useful knowledge about cooking."

"It's the sweetest, dearest little kitchen in the world. I would rather learn all about it and all the things I can make in it than anything else in the world," Daisy said. She promptly put on the little apron and cap that were hanging with great care beside the stove and got to work.

She and her aunt played for hours, and even went to "market" downstairs in Asia's well-run kitchen.

"Now put everything away in your cupboard," Jo said with a smile, for there was another surprise. When Daisy opened up the cupboard doors, she saw all kinds of small jars filled up with anything she might need: flour, sugar, corn meal, and even two sweet little doll-sized milk pans with fresh milk.

After a while, the boys all clamored outside the door to see what was going on. Once they were allowed in, they set about inspecting every inch of the stove and the little kitchen. Demi offered to buy her boiler on the spot, for it would make a very good addition to the steam engine he was building. And when Tommy saw the large saucepan, he declared it would be just perfect to melt lead.

Aunt Jo stood back and declared that no boy could touch the stove or the pieces of the little kitchen without Daisy saying it was okay.

"None of these items will ever be for sale, either. Am I making myself clear?" Jo said sternly.

Before long, the day was over and it was time for bed. As Jo tucked Daisy into bed, she asked her if she liked her kitchen.

"Oh, it's the dearest game ever made!"

"What shall we call it?" Jo asked. "For every game needs a name."

"You name it, Aunt Jo. It was you who came up with it and had it built, even if Uncle Laurie did help a great deal."

"Fine, fine," Jo thought for a moment. "We'll call it Patty-Pans—after the nursery rhyme."

"It's perfect, Aunt Jo," Daisy said as she drifted off to sleep, "just perfect."

# CHAPTER 6

# Another New Boy!

❦

Jo was sitting in her parlor with a book when Nat came to see her one afternoon. His was the fifth head to pop in that afternoon, but Jo didn't mind the interruptions. The boy stepped inside, shut the door behind him, and said, "Dan has come."

Jo set her book down and asked, "Who is Dan?"

"He's a boy I used to know when I fiddled on the streets," Nat answered. "He sold papers and was kind to me, and I saw him the other day in town. I told him how nice it is here, and he's come."

Jo looked startled for a moment. "But, dear me, it's a very sudden way to pay a visit."

"Oh, he hasn't come for a visit," Nat answered. "He's come to stay."

Jo explained that he couldn't possibly stay, as they had no room for even one more boy. But when she came to the end of her speech, Nat looked so upset with himself for making a mistake that Jo sat him down on the stool beside her chair.

"Now tell me about this Dan," she said.

"All I know is that he doesn't have any folks, and he's poor, and he was good to me when we were on the streets, so I'd like to be good to him if I can."

Jo said, "Excellent reasons, every one. But really, we have so many boys at Plumfield that I wouldn't even know where to put him."

"He could stay in my bed, and I'll sleep in the

barn," Nat offered. "It's not that cold, and I used to sleep anywhere with Father."

Something in his face made Jo put her hand on his shoulder and say kindly, "Bring in your friend, Nat. I think we must find room for him, but you will not be sleeping in the barn."

Nat raced off to find the lad. When they came back in, Jo knew instantly that she did not trust him. "Nat says that you would like to come and stay with us," she said.

A rough-looking Dan mumbled, "Yes."

"Have you no friends to take care of you?"

"No," he said in a gruff voice.

"How old are you?" Jo asked.

"Fourteen."

Nat whispered, "You should say 'ma'am.'"

"Shan't neither," Dan hissed back.

Jo pretended not to hear them. "Has Nat told you that in order to stay here, you'll need to work and study hard? Are you willing?"

45

"I don't mind trying," Dan said.

"Well, I suppose you can stay for a few days, and we'll see how it goes."

Nat smiled. "Take him outside and introduce him to all the boys until Father Bhaer comes home, and then we'll settle the matter," Jo said.

"Come on, Nat," said a scowling Dan as they left the room.

"Thank you, ma'am," Nat said. When they were outside, he added, "We're setting up a circus in the barn, if you want to come and see."

Dan shrugged his shoulders and mumbled, "Sure."

When they arrived, the circus was almost complete. The boys had set up a large circle of hay in the middle of the floor. Nat introduced Dan to everyone, and the pair sat down to watch the show.

Tommy pranced around the inside of the circle atop poor old Toby, who neighed the entire time. Demi was the circus master and carried a large whip, while two of the other boys wrestled in the center. To end the performance, Tommy did a somersault, which he had practiced until he was black and blue.

"Harrumph," Dan said. "That ain't anything."

Tommy stood before him and shouted, "Say that again, will you?"

Dan held up his fists. "Do you want to fight about it?"

"No, I don't," Tommy said and stepped away. One of the other boys shouted, "Fighting isn't allowed, so stop that now!"

"You're a bunch of silly boys," Dan replied.

Nat stepped forward and put a hand on his friend's shoulder. "Come on. If you don't behave, Mother Jo won't let you stay."

"I'd just like to see him do the somersault better than I can, that's all," Tommy insisted.

Dan sneered. "Fine."

Before Tommy could say another word, Dan turned three somersaults in a row and then walked on his hands. When he stood back up, an impressed Tommy asked, "Will you teach me to do that?"

"What will you give me?" Dan replied.

Tommy told Dan that he had a good pocket-knife, which he handed over.

"Ha! When you learn, I'll give it back."

Outraged, the boys protested so much at Dan's bad behavior that he ended up handing Tommy's knife back to him before Nat pulled him outside. No one ever knew what passed between the two of them, but when they returned, Dan was nicer to all the boys.

Still, he was rough in his manners and almost impossible to control. Tommy pushed hard, and the two became close over the issue of somersaults. But the rest of the boys simply did not like Dan. Of everyone, it was because little Teddy took such a liking to Dan that Jo became determined to find the good in the boy.

Even though she lost her patience with him day after day, Jo never gave up. She saw Dan with Teddy and knew he had a softer side.

Dan thought the rule about fighting was silly, and as the weeks went on, he often teased the boys about it. One day, he gathered everyone behind the barn and began to teach them how to box. Dan was fighting with one of the older boys when Father Bhaer found them.

He plucked them apart with a strong hand and said, "I can't allow this, boys! Stop it at once and never let me see it again. We keep a school for boys, not for animals."

"Let me at him. I'll knock him down again," Dan shouted as Father Bhaer held tight to his collar.

"They're playing gladdy-somethings, Uncle Bhaer," Demi said.

"Gladiators. They were a fine set of brutes that had no choice but to fight," Father Bhaer said. "And you'll not turn my barn into the Roman Colosseum, where they fought. Whose idea was it to do battle?"

Several voices answered, "Dan's."

Father Bhaer turned to the boy and asked, "Why did you break the rules?"

"They'll all be ninnies if they don't learn how to fight," Dan replied.

Father Bhaer pulled the two boys in close so they could see exactly what they had done to one another. Dan had a black eye and his jacket had been torn to rags. The other boy's face was covered in blood from a cut lip, and he had a bruised nose and a big bump on his forehead that was already as purple as a plum.

"You both look like fine ninnies right now," Father Bhaer said, and then he sent all the boys up to their rooms so they could think about what they had done. Before he let Dan go, he spoke to him at length about why it was important to obey the rules. When they came back inside, Father Bhaer believed the boy had finally learned his lesson.

But less than a week later, Dan found himself in trouble again. This time, he had encouraged the boys to play bull-fights. They teased the old cow, Buttercup, by riding Toby around and around her. When she became tired and angry with their teasing, Buttercup broke the fence and charged away to hide in the flower beds. Even though they got her back in the pen, and no real damage was done to poor old Toby, Father Bhaer grew angry when he learned of the incident. The longer Dan sat on his bed awaiting his punishment, the more he thought about how much he wanted to stay at Plumfield. Being grateful had never been easy for him, and now he felt he had made one mistake too many.

Finally Father Bhaer came in and said, "I have heard all about it, Dan, and even though you have broken the rules again, we are going to give you one more chance."

"I didn't know there was any rule about pretend bull fighting," Dan said.

Father Bhaer answered patiently, "I shouldn't have thought that I would have to make a rule. You are always so kind to animals. You should have known that using them for play would turn out this way. You have disappointed us by treating those creatures so poorly. But shall we try one more time to be good?"

Dan looked at the floor and said quietly, "Yes, please."

"Good. Tomorrow you will stay back from the walk with the other boys and take care of Buttercup until she is well again."

Dan did his best to be good for the next few days, but he just couldn't help himself. One day

Father Bhaer was called into town for business and their lessons were cancelled. The boys were excited about a day spent outside playing, and they were wound up until well after lunch. Mother Jo was tied up with Teddy, who had a bad cough, so the boys were on their own. Dan decided to teach them how to play cards.

There was so much excitement around the game that when a small fight broke out, no one noticed the old lantern fall to the floor and set the curtains on fire. The blaze spread so quickly that they barely had time to call, "Fire! Fire!"

Franz smelled the smoke and burst into the room, pulling the boys out as quickly as possible. Asia tended to the burns while

53

the uninjured boys worked hard to stop the flames from spreading. By the end of it all, Demi had a small burn on his back and Tommy had lost most of his hair and burned his arm terribly. The pain made him miserable, and Jo looked after him for most of the night.

There were no lessons again the next day, and the boys spent much of the morning putting the house back together. Burned curtains were replaced and new beds were made. When Father Bhaer finally sat the boys down to find out what had happened, he found that all but Dan were willing to apologize. Father Bhaer could not believe the boys were up to so much mischief.

"I think that Tommy has learned his lesson, and Nat's been scared enough, but you, Dan, we've forgiven you time and time again. Asia will pack your things into my old black bag and we'll take you away to Mr. Page's school far out in the country."

"Will he ever come back, Uncle Bhaer?" Demi asked.

"That will depend on him. I hope so. If he improves and Mr. Page decides he can return to Plumfield," Father Bhaer answered.

With that, he left the room to write a letter to the other school. The boys crowded around poor Dan.

"I wonder if you'll like it," Nat said.

"Shan't stay if I don't," Dan answered.

"Oh, don't be that way," Nat pleaded. "Where would you go?"

"Anywhere, really. California, maybe, or to the sea. I don't care where I go or how long I stay because I'm never coming back here. That's something I know for sure!"

Dan left the room then to pack up the rest of his things, all of which had been given to him by the boys, Father Bhaer, and Mother Jo. Dan's outburst was the only good-bye he gave the boys, for when they came downstairs, he was already gone. Jo had allowed Dan one last moment to say good-bye to his precious Teddy, and that was it. His pride would not let him ask for one last chance, even though his heart called out for it, and Dan left Plumfield with a hard look on his face.

The boys rejoiced when a letter arrived from Mr. Page a few days later saying that the boy was doing well. But then, with the next letter, they learned that he had run away.

After lights-out, Father Bhaer said to Jo quietly, "Perhaps we should have given him one last chance."

"Don't fret, dear. The boy will come back to us. I'm sure of it."

But Jo's heart was heavy as she fell asleep that night wishing that Dan *would* come back to them sooner rather than later. Plumfield just wasn't the same without him.

CHAPTER 7

# Here Comes Naughty Nan

⁓

One day when Dan had been gone for almost a month, Jo met Father Bhaer after school and said, "I have an idea."

Father Bhaer smiled. "Well, my dear, what is it?"

"Daisy needs a friend to play with. You know that as well as I do, and I think the boys have been quite sad with Dan gone. We need to find a new student. The boys might be on better behavior if we have another girl around, so I think we should ask Nan Harding to stay."

Father Bhaer laughed and said, "Naughty Nan?"

"Yes," Jo insisted. "She's been running wild since her mother passed away. It would do the boys a world of good. I know her father would like her to come to Plumfield—I asked him the other day while I was in town."

Father Bhaer bent his head and considered his wife. Jo continued, "I think it'll be good for Daisy as well. She's getting too prim and proper here by herself. And she'll help Nan not to be so wild."

"That does make sense," Father Bhaer agreed. "My only worry is that Nan will turn into another firecracker like Dan."

"So shall I tell Nan to come and stay?" Jo asked.

"Of course, dear, of course!"

The next day Jo returned to Plumfield with more than her usual packages from town. A small ten-year-old girl jumped down from the wagon and burst into the house shouting, "Hello, Daisy! Where are you?"

Daisy came out to greet her guest.

"I'm here to stay," Nan shouted. "Papa says I must, and your aunt came to carry me away, and my box comes tomorrow, and isn't it great fun?"

Daisy nodded slowly and watched as Nan danced around her. Daisy asked quietly, "Did you bring your big doll?"

"Oh, yes. She's around somewhere, and I even brought you this bracelet that I wove just 'cause I know we didn't part on the best of terms when I was here last. But all that's going to change now that I'm here full-time. It's going to be grand."

Daisy thanked Nan for the friendship bracelet, and Nan shouted, "Let's go see the boys out in the barn!"

With that, Nan skipped off, swinging her hat with such might that it broke off from its strings and was left behind where it landed in the grass. Daisy followed reluctantly behind her.

"Hullo, boys!" Nan shouted. "I'm going to stay!"

The boys cheered as she came up to stand beside Tommy, who was sitting on the fence trying very hard not to cry. A ball and bat were on the grass beneath his feet.

Nan shoved him a little on the shoulder. "Come on, I'll play. I can hit the ball pretty far, and it's a nice day for it. What's wrong with you?"

"We're not playing anymore. The ball hurt my hand," Tommy sniffed.

"I don't cry about anything. It's babyish," Nan said.

Tommy sniffed again and said, "Go and pick a bunch of nettles then, if you're so strong."

"I will," Nan said as she stomped over to a nettle plant, grabbed it, and held on for dear life regardless of the sting.

"Pooh, you're just used to it," Tommy said. "Now go and run your head into the barn, then you'll cry."

Nan did just that, and her head hit the barn with such a crack that Tommy thought for sure she would cry. But when Nan stood back up, her face was dry. The boys just stood and stared. They didn't know whether to be shocked or impressed, for who runs their head into a barn?

"Ho, I don't mind, because I ain't a little girl, and it didn't hurt much." Nan pressed her hand to her forehead where a terrible bruise had already started to form. Just then the dinner bell rang, and all the children trooped back to the house.

When Father Bhaer asked for Nan's hand so he could say grace, she told him that it hurt too much. Before long, the whole story of the nettles and the barn came out. Father Bhaer looked to his wife with a smile in his eyes and said, "Perhaps this is one for you to handle."

Jo smiled at the boys and said, "Do you know why I asked Nan to come to school here?"

"To torture me," Tommy said.

"No, to help make little gentlemen out of you. I think you've shown that you do need it, after all."

Tommy bent his head down over his plate as Demi shouted, "How can she help us? She's such a tomboy!"

Jo answered, "That's just it—she needs as much help as you do."

"Will she become a gentleman, too?" Jo's son, Rob, asked.

Tommy laughed and said, "You'd like that, wouldn't you, Nan?"

Nan's hand and head hurt, and for a moment she thought she should have shown her courage in other ways. "No, I wouldn't! I hate boys."

Jo laughed. "Well, I'm sorry if you do hate

them, but they are usually well-mannered and most agreeable and treat everyone kindly."

She looked right at Nan and continued, "They've all learned the lesson that you treat other people the way you wish to be treated yourself."

For the rest of dinner, the boys took Jo's hint and were on their best behavior. Nan kept to herself, even though she desperately wanted to tickle Demi for teasing her.

The next morning, Nan could not sit still. She wanted to know when her box was going to arrive. Jo said that it should get there at some point during the day, but that wasn't enough for Nan. She paced back and forth, fretting and fuming until after lunch, when she disappeared.

"I'll bet she's run off home!" Jo said.

"She was going on about her luggage all day," Franz replied. "Maybe she's gone to the station."

Jo shook her head. "Oh, the foolish girl. The box would be far too heavy for her to carry, and she doesn't even know the way!"

The entire house was about to set off in search of Nan when Franz shouted, "Here she comes!"

And indeed, there was Nan, tugging her giant box behind her and kicking up all kinds of dust along the way. Father Bhaer helped her with the last few steps and placed the box on the porch by the front door. Nan sat down, folded her arms, and said, "I couldn't wait any longer, so I went to get it."

"But you didn't know the way," Tommy said.

"Oh, I found it," Nan replied. "I *never* get lost." She wiped her dusty forehead with her sleeve and sat there looking at everyone.

"How could you go so far by yourself?" Tommy asked, amazed. "And all the way back carrying that box!"

"I did think my arms would break . . ."

"I don't see how the station master let you have it," Franz insisted.

"I didn't say anything to him," Nan said. "I just took it off the platform. He didn't see me because he was in the ticket booth."

Father Bhaer asked Franz to run down to the station and tell the old station master what had happened before he thought the box stolen. Jo wiped Nan's dusty face and told her never to run away again. To this Nan replied, "I can't promise—my papa has always told me not to put off doing things, and so I don't."

The boys had great fun at dinner listening to the story of Nan's adventure. On the way back to Plumfield, a big dog had barked at her, a man had laughed at her, a woman had given her a doughnut, and her hat had fallen into a brook when she had stopped for a drink.

Once all the children had settled into bed for the night, Father Bhaer said to Jo, "It seems like you might have your hands full with Tommy and Nan."

Jo laughed. "I know it will take some time for her learn new ways, but she has such a good heart."

The next day, Nan only proved Jo right as she opened up her box and shared her belongings with all the children. Soon, it was as if Plumfield had never existed without her, nor been so lively.

# CHAPTER 8

# Daisy's Ball

One day, the boys were all sitting around just waiting for something to happen when an invitation came from Daisy:

> *Mrs. Shakespeare Smith would like to have*
> *Mr. John Brooke (Demi), Mr. Thomas Banks*
> *(Tommy), and Mr. Nathaniel Blake (Nat) come*
> *to her ball at three o'clock today.*
>
> *P.S. Nat must bring his fiddle so we can dance,*
> *and all the boys must behave, or they cannot have the*
> *goodies we have cooked.*

After a careful inspection of the paper, Tommy said, "The girls have been cooking lots of goodies. I've smelled them. Why don't we go?"

"I've never been to a ball. What do you do?" Nat asked.

"Oh, we'll just play at being gentlemen and dance to please the girls. Then we can eat the goodies," Tommy said.

"I'll write and say that we'll come," Demi replied and quickly jotted down:

*We will all come. Please have lots to eat.*

*—J.B., Esquire.*

Meanwhile, Daisy and Nan were nervously buzzing about the nursery, preparing for the ball.

"Demi and Nat will be good, I know they will. But Tommy will do something bad. He always does, even though he doesn't mean to," Nan said.

Daisy set the table and looked around at all

the treats they had prepared in her little kitchen. "I shall send him away if he does, and we'll never ask him again."

When the table was finished, both girls got into their costumes. As the lady of the house, Daisy's outfit was plain—only a red night cap with a bow to cover her head. Nan wore a wreath of artificial flowers, a pair of old pink slippers, a yellow scarf, a green muslin skirt, and a fan made of feathers from the duster.

She said, "I'm more dressed up 'cause I'm the daughter and you are the mother. I'll dance and talk more than you. The mothers only get the tea and have to be proper."

Just then, a loud knock on the nursery door signaled that it was time for the party to begin. The door opened and there stood the boys wearing paper collars, tall black hats, and unmatched gloves of every color and material!

"Good day, ma'am," Demi said in a very low voice that was hard to keep without hurting his throat.

Everyone shook hands and then sat down looking so serious that the boys broke out in laughter.

"Oh, please don't," Daisy said.

Nan added, "You shall never come again if you keep laughing at us."

Tommy giggled. "I can't help it. You look so funny."

"So do you," Nan replied, "but I won't be so rude as to say so. You'll have to leave if you can't be nice, right Daisy?"

Wanting to keep the peace, Daisy said to Nat, "Why don't you get your fiddle, and we'll have our dance now."

The boys protested and asked to have dinner first, hoping to be able to leave before the dancing began, but they had no such luck. As Nat played, the two couples did the best they could, with the girls tripping over their costumes and the boys taking the wrong step more often than the right one.

When they were all out of breath, the group sat back down at the table, and Daisy served everyone molasses and water. Tommy helped himself to nine cups!

"Now you need to ask Nan to sing," Daisy whispered to Demi.

He cleared his throat, dropped his voice, and said politely, "How about a song?"

Nan sprung into action and promptly sang three pretty songs for the boys, who clapped with great energy when she finished.

"Now we shall have the meal," Daisy said as she proudly served up the custard she had made. It was so runny that they ended up having to drink it. Then it was time for the final course: raisin tarts. Only they were missing!

"You've got them, Tommy. I know you do," Nan said.

"I haven't."

"I can see them in your pockets!" she shouted.

"Come on, let's give them back," Demi said. But Tommy wouldn't have it—it was too much fun to keep them. Nat, who had been enjoying himself a great deal, pounced forward and started to chase Tommy around the room. Soon there were pieces of tart flying every which way. Daisy started to cry as Nat and Demi finally caught a laughing Tommy and threw him out of the nursery.

"I guess we had better go," Demi said.

"Perhaps we had," Nat added.

The boys were not quite out of the nursery before Jo arrived. The girls poured out the story of the ruined ball.

"No more balls for these boys until they have

made it up to you," she said as she shook her head at the boys.

"But we were just having fun," Demi said.

"But you shouldn't have fun at other people's expense. And it's not nice to tease the girls after they went to so much trouble to throw you a party," Jo added. "Daisy is such a good sister to you, I had hoped you would be kinder to her."

Demi pouted. "Boys *always* tease their sisters. Tommy says so."

Jo looked stern. "I don't want you to tease Daisy. If you can't play nicely with her, I'll send her home."

Demi did not want to be parted from Daisy, so he put his arm around his sister's shoulder and apologized.

"I'm sorry, too," Nat said.

"I'm not!" Tommy shouted from the other side of the door.

Jo wanted very much to laugh, but she kept a straight face. "You boys can go now, but you will not be allowed to have any more balls. In fact, you're to keep entirely away from the girls until I say so."

Over the next few days, the boys pretended not to care about their punishment, but they soon missed the company of Nan and Daisy. Even Jo was keeping her distance to truly make the point. When they could stand it no longer, they asked Father Bhaer for help. Jo had given her husband an idea of what to say, and he encouraged the boys to make it up to the girls in one particular way.

The boys locked themselves away in a room for several hours while the curious girls tried to look through the windows. Nan almost got her nose caught in the door as they tried to find out what the boys were doing. When Nat and Tommy went off with a very large package wrapped in newspaper, the girls' curiosity almost got the best of them. They simply *had* to know what was in the package! They tried everything to get the boys to tell them—but they kept quiet.

Later on that afternoon, Demi came into Jo's parlor with his cap in hand. "Aunt Jo," he said, "would you and the girls please come out to a surprise party we have made for you?"

Jo smiled and said, "Thank you. I would love to come."

"The wagon's all ready for the girls, and you won't mind walking up to Pennyroyal Hill, will you?"

Jo said, "I should like it very much, but are you sure I won't be in the way?"

Demi said proudly, "We want you to come most of all!" He quickly ran back outside to tell the other boys, who were all hiding, that the girls would soon be on their way.

The girls rushed about collecting their hats,

and five minutes later, they were all tucked into the little wagon that Toby pulled behind him. The boys had even dressed him up in a feather duster and attached flags to the wagon. Franz, who was driving the wagon, made sure they found the exact spot where the boys had set up the party.

When the girls arrived at the top of the hill, they couldn't see the boys anywhere. In a matter of seconds, the boys came out from behind the rocks carrying beautiful new kites, which they gave to the girls. Daisy and Nan squealed in delight.

"But that's not all!" Tommy shouted as he ran behind the rock again and returned with both Father Bhaer and another kite they had made for Mother Jo.

Soon, the boys were showing the girls how to fly their kites, and all the merry little contraptions floated on the wind. They had a marvelous afternoon. They played and laughed until dinnertime, when they made their way back down the hill to Plumfield. All was right again between the girls and the boys, who had finally been forgiven for ruining the ball.

# CHAPTER 9

# Home Again

～

Now that it was summer, the boys' classes were shorter, and they spent a lot of time outside. The garden came along nicely, and they helped with the weeding. Plumfield stood open from morning until night to welcome all home at a moment's notice.

One balmy night as Jo was putting Teddy to bed, he said in his baby voice, "Oh, my Danny!" and pointed to the window.

Jo said, "No my dear, he is not there. It's just the moon."

"No, no, my Danny at the window, at the window," Teddy shouted as he bounced up and down.

Jo scooped up her little boy and raced to the front door, hoping to see Dan. She even called out to him, but there was no one there.

It was almost ten o'clock when Jo went to lock up the house for the night. As she looked around, something caught her eye—a dash of white out in the front yard. The children had been playing out there this afternoon, and Jo thought that Nan must have left her hat outside. But when she went out to retrieve it, she found Dan, fast asleep on the lawn. One of his feet was bare, and the other was tied up in an old gingham jacket.

"He must not lie here," Jo said, and she shook him softly as she called out his name.

"Mother Jo," Dan mumbled, "I've come home."

Jo smiled and said, "We are very glad to see you."

Dan stirred. "I had planned just to stop by and be on my way in the morning," he said.

"Why don't you come in? Everyone would love to see you, especially Teddy. Didn't you hear him calling you?"

Dan hung his head. "I didn't suppose you'd let me in."

Jo held out her hand to help him up, for he had hurt his foot badly. As he leaned on an old stick, Dan said, "Father Bhaer will not be pleased with me. I've run away from Mr. Page."

"He knows," Jo said. "He was sorry to hear it, but he'll still be happy you are home. Now, what happened to your foot?"

"As I was climbing over a stone wall, one large rock came loose and fell on me," Dan replied. "It's not that bad, and I don't mind."

But Jo could see that he was in an awful lot of pain. She helped him into her parlor and gave him something to eat and drink. Once he was settled in, Dan told her about all of his unhappy adventures.

When she left the room for more bandages, Jo found Father Bhaer and told him of Dan's hard times since leaving them. Father Bhaer said at once that the boy should stay. Dan overheard everything and allowed just two tears to fall down his face. All his anger was now behind him. He had never been so happy to be home.

"But do go and tend to his foot, my dear," Jo said. "I am afraid it is badly hurt. And be kind to him. He's had a hard time of it."

Father Bhaer smiled at his wife and gave her a quick kiss on the cheek. Then he went in to see Dan. "So you like Plumfield better than Page's farm?" he said kindly. "Let's make sure we get along better this time around."

"Thank you, sir," Dan said without a hint of the old gruffness in his voice.

Father Bhaer took a good look at Dan's foot and said they must call for the doctor in the morning, and then he bandaged it up tightly.

The next morning, Teddy found Dan and ran toward him with a huge smile on his little face. The doctor came that afternoon to set the bones in his foot right, which Dan bore with great bravery. The doctor was pleased because it wasn't a bad break and should heal well. Soon the boys were allowed in to see Dan, and he told them all about his adventures, careful not to make them sound too grand, for nothing was better than life at Plumfield.

The boys were so happy to have Dan back, for they all had missed him very much. But no one was happier than Jo. She saw a great change in the boy, and he made Teddy so happy that her heart soared just to think of it.

On her way upstairs after settling Dan in for a night's sleep in the parlor, she thought, *He's finally made a turn for the better—although I suspect it will be hard for him to be entirely good* all *the time.*

# CHAPTER 10

## Uncle Laurie's Visit

Dan spent an entire week recovering. He moved from sofa to bed and rested even though he longed to be outside in the warm summer weather.

The doctor came by late the next Sunday afternoon and said, "The foot is doing much better than I expected. Give the lad a crutch and let him move around a little."

Everyone was very glad, and after dinner the entire house stood together to watch Dan walk with the crutch up and down the hallway. He tired after a few steps, so he settled on the porch with the boys at his feet. He was pleased by the attention and smiled as the girls fussed over his pillows. Little Teddy even dragged out a stool for him to rest his foot on.

A large group of people was already gathered outside the house when a carriage drove up and an arm waved from the gate.

Rob cried out, "Uncle Laurie!" and ran down the drive as fast as his small legs would take him. The rest of the boys (except Dan, of course) followed close behind. They raced to see who could open the gate first. Uncle Laurie just laughed and bounced his daughter, Bess, on his knee.

He shouted in good fun, "Hey, ho! Let a man get down!"

Jo stood with her hands on her hips and a big smile on her face. "How goes it, Laurie?"

"All right, Jo."

They shook hands and Laurie handed Bess over to Jo. He said, "Bessy wanted to see her aunt so much that we raced right over. We've decided to play with the boys for an hour or so . . . if they don't have any other plans."

"I'm so glad," Jo said. "Do play away, but don't get into mischief."

The warning was, of course, for the boys, who crowded around sweet Bess with her long, golden hair, dainty dress, and lofty ways. They called her "princess" and did her bidding at all times. Bess wished to see Daisy's little kitchen, so off they went upstairs. The older boys went out into the garden to make sure everything was tip-top, as Laurie always had a good look around.

Standing on the steps, Laurie said to Dan, "Jo told me all about your accident. How is the foot?"

"It's much better, sir."

"Getting tired of the house?" Laurie asked.

Dan let his eyes wander over to the green hills and answered, "I guess I am!"

"Why don't we take a quick ride in the carriage? The fresh air will do you good."

Laurie asked Demi to get another cushion and a jacket for Dan. "Are you sure Mother Jo won't mind?" the boy asked.

"Oh, I'm sure it'll be fine," Laurie said. "Trust me."

In a few minutes Dan was settled in the carriage, his foot tucked in so it wouldn't get hurt. Demi, Nat, and Laurie all climbed aboard, and they were well on their way before the older gentleman took a funny little stone from his pocket to show the boys.

"Look here," he said, "it's a beetle that's thousands of years old."

"How did it get like this?" Nat marveled as he turned the gray stone over in his hand.

"Why, it's a mummy," Laurie answered. He

went on to tell the boys stories of the Egyptians and their tombs with all the great treasures to be found within. Laurie had just returned from a trip to Egypt. He was full of the adventure, and the boys hung on his every word. Soon, Nat, Dan, and Demi were pulling objects out of their pockets, showing them to one another and telling stories.

"You know," Laurie said, "I think it's a good idea for you boys to have a museum of your own—a place to keep all your treasures so you can always show them to one another."

"But there's no room at Plumfield," Demi said. "Where would we set it up?"

"Ah, I've already thought about that," Laurie answered. "Father Bhaer and I are going to fix up the old carriage house for you. Won't that be grand?"

The three boys all agreed that it absolutely would. They had arrived back at Plumfield by now, and the driver asked if they would like to go around again. Laurie told him that Dan needed his rest, and even though the boys would have loved to go around again, they knew the ride had come to an end.

Once Dan was safely settled back on the porch, Laurie walked through the garden and examined all the boys' hard work. By the time he was done, Jo had found her way outside.

Laurie sat down at a stool with the boys and said, "You know, Dan, I was the head boy at this school once."

"Wait!" Dan said, "I thought that was Franz."

"Oh, no," Laurie said. "I was the very first boy Jo ever took care of, and she's still not done, even though she's been working on me for years and years."

They all laughed. "You see," he continued, "she was only fifteen when she started. I've caused her so much trouble, it's a wonder she's not old, wrinkled, and gray!"

"Oh, Laurie," Jo said. "Don't be so silly! If it hadn't been for you, there would be no Plumfield. I think we should rename the old carriage house 'The Laurence Museum.' How does that sound, boys?"

Shouts of "great!" and "hooray!" rose up all around. When they finally died down, Laurie said, "Jo, I'm starving—how about we all have a snack? Apples? Cookies? Anything!"

Just as Jo was about to send Demi to the kitchen to ask Asia for snack, Laurie jumped up and ran to the carriage. "Hold on!" he shouted.

When he returned, he was carrying a lovely white package. "They're gingerbread cookies that your mother made, Jo. She would have been very upset with me had I forgotten to share them!"

The gingerbread was passed around from boy to boy, and each took a piece. Each cookie was in a shape that delighted a particular boy: Nat's was a fiddle, Demi's a book, and Tommy's a monkey.

As he brushed the crumbs off his hands, Laurie said, "Well, my hour's almost up. Has anyone seen my princess?"

At just that second, Nan tore around the corner at a breakneck pace, chasing a team of four boys pretending to be horses. Daisy followed swiftly behind with little Bess in a wheelbarrow.

"That's them now," Jo said with a worried tone in her voice. "And just as we thought Nan was becoming more ladylike."

Laurie shouted, "What on earth are you doing?" He lifted Bess up out of the wheelbarrow and looked at them sternly.

Daisy said breathlessly, "We were having a race. I would have won, too, but I was worried about spilling Bessy from the wheelbarrow."

"I won!" Nan shouted.

Jo and Laurie both shook their heads as the girls raced off again, leaving Bess behind.

"Good-bye, Jo," Laurie said. "And good luck!"

In just one short week, The Laurence Museum was up and running in the old carriage house. The boys spent an afternoon inside finding homes for all their boyish treasures: rocks, bugs, snake skins, and all manner of objects that captured their attention.

Laurie returned for the official opening ceremony and gave a lovely speech about how the boys weren't just to collect things, but to learn all about their objects as well. He named Dan keeper of the museum, which pleased the boy to no end. Father Bhaer even gave him a lovely book all about insects so he could teach the other boys.

After the boys went back to the house to wash for dinner, Laurie stood back with Jo and said, "Jo, I have known what it's like to be a motherless boy. I will never forget how much you and yours have done for me all these years."

No more words were necessary as Jo patted her dear friend's hand and they went back up to the house for the celebration.

# CHAPTER 11

# The Huckleberry Adventure

ᘓ

One day late in the summer, the boys decided to go huckleberry picking. A great clashing of pails could be heard all over Plumfield as they prepared for their adventure. Jo laughed to herself. They were making so much fuss, they may as well have been setting out to find the Northwest Passage.

"Now," she said to them, "Rob's safely out of the way, so get off as quickly as you can."

But the boys weren't quiet enough, and little

Rob heard the noise and came scampering toward them, pail in hand.

*Oh dear,* Jo thought. *Now we'll have a scene.*

She stepped forward and called out, "Come now, Rob. It's too far to go. You stay back with me."

Rob pouted. "You said I could go when I was bigger. Now I am bigger."

"It's very far," Tommy said, "and you might get tired. Better that you stay back."

"I won't get tired!" Rob insisted. "I'll run, and I'll keep up, and I'll fill my pail, and I'll bring all the berries to you."

The little boy's smile had all but disappeared.

"Oh, please," he said. "I really want to go, and I won't get tired. I won't."

Giant tears fell out of his eyes. Jo couldn't stand the sight of any one of her boys being unhappy, and so an idea came to her.

"Wait here, boys! I think I have a solution. One that will mean even Dan can go!"

The boys stood holding their pans while Jo raced back into the house. When she came back a few minutes later, she had a huge smile on her face.

"Franz will take you up the hill in the wagon and then pick you up at the end of the day. Dan, you may go as well. And be sure to let the girls take good care of you. Nan, you're to keep an eye on Rob."

Rob threw himself on his mother in a fit of gratitude and promised to bring her back every berry he picked. Soon they were all packed into the wagon, with Rob, pleased as punch, snuggled in between Nan and Daisy.

What a happy day they had—even if the picking didn't necessarily go as planned! Tommy fell into a hornet's nest and was stung, but being used to such woes, he bore it gracefully. Daisy saw a snake, and it scared her so much that she threw her bucket in the air and lost most of her berries. Being a kind brother, Demi helped her fill it back up again. And Dan, who no longer needed his crutch, walked quietly among the hills and bushes, happy that his foot felt so much better.

But of all the adventures that happened that afternoon, the one that Nan and Rob found themselves in, became one of Plumfield's best-loved stories. Having explored far and wide, torn her dress in three different places, and scratched her face while scrambling around in a barberry bush, Nan turned her attention to the huckleberries. The big, black, bead-like berries hung low on the green bushes. When her basket didn't fill quickly enough, Nan moved to a new bush, with little Rob in tow.

"I'm so tired!" Rob said as his bucket toppled over. "I can't fill it up. It's just too much."

Looking around, Nan said, "Look, there's a cave over there—why don't we go hide and make everyone come looking for us? We can pick more berries on the way."

And away they went, scrambling over a low stone wall and running down the hill until they were hidden among rocks and brush. They came across a little spring, and the two thirsty children drank a bit of cool water. The shade was a relief after gathering berries in the hot sun.

"Now let's go rest in the cave and have our lunch," Nan said.

Rob asked, "Do you know the way back to the huckleberry field?"

"Of course I do!" Nan answered.

And so the unlikely pair set off, with Rob scrambling to keep up with the quick Nan. They soon came to the cave Nan had spied earlier.

"Isn't this nice?" Nan asked as she took out their lunch.

"Yes," Rob nodded, and he took a bite of bread. "Do you think it'll take them long to find us?"

"They'll be here soon. I can feel it!" Nan replied.

Rob looked around at the gloomy cave and said, "What if they don't come?"

"Then we'll find our way back on our own."

Little five-year-old Rob was very tired, and he wanted very much to find everyone and take the wagon home. But he sat and waited patiently while Nan left the cave to gather even more berries.

The sun started to set, and a mosquito bit him. Then the frogs started to sing their evening songs.

"Perhaps it will be dark soon?" Rob called out.

Nan looked up from where she had been roaming about and noticed that it was indeed getting dark. "My, we'd better get going right away, or they will be gone!"

She pulled Rob along behind her, back up the hill. But as they came to the top, she wondered which way to go next. Rob pointed his finger in exactly the wrong direction, and that was the path they took. Over rock and stone, they listened for Franz's horn. But they didn't hear it—not once!

"I don't remember that pile of stones," Nan said. "Do you?"

"I remember none, and I want to go home," Rob cried as he sat down on the ground in a tired fit. Nan soon sat next to him.

"Oh, don't cry. I'm going as fast as I can. When we get to the road, I'll carry you."

Rob stuttered, "W-w-where is the road?"

"Over by that big tree—don't you remember? It's the one Nat fell out of."

They picked themselves up and trudged through a large pasture. But when they got to the tree, they found that there was no road, nor was it the right tree.

"I think maybe we should shout," Nan suggested.

They did as Nan said and hollered until their throats were dry and hoarse.

"We are lost," Rob sobbed.

"Only a little," Nan replied. "We can bunk here tonight and find our way home tomorrow."

"I want to be home now!"

Nan tried to comfort Rob by telling him all the fun things they could find to eat. They even tried to light a fire by catching fireflies, which certainly didn't work. When they tried to walk a

bit farther, Rob was so tired that he stumbled more than he stepped. Nan suggested he lie down with his head in her lap, and she pulled her apron on top of him. Soon, both children were fast asleep.

Meanwhile, the boys had noticed that Nan and Rob were missing and set out to look for them. The search team consisted of mainly the older boys, including Franz, Nat, Dan, and Tommy. The wagon made a good circle of the area and arrived back at Plumfield.

"Have they returned?" Franz shouted.

Jo came running out. "No!"

Franz pulled up in front of the porch and said, "I can't find them anywhere."

Jo turned to Demi. "Go and get Uncle Bhaer, and tell him to bring the lanterns. We must get everyone out looking."

Franz set out again on the horse while Dan rode on Toby and Jo and Father Bhaer went on foot. The moon was out now, and lanterns could be seen up and down the fields.

"They could have gone down to the spring," Dan shouted. "I'll go and see what I can find."

When they heard Dan shout again, the entire search party made their way over to him.

"I can see little footprints here!" he said.

A little farther on, Nan's hat and the top of a berry pail appeared. Dan rode Toby out farther into the field and soon discovered Nan and Rob fast asleep on the other side of a big tree.

"They're over here!" he shouted, and soon the whole search party gathered around. Rob's sleepy eyes opened and he shouted, "Mama! Mama! I knew you would come and find me!"

Jo hugged her little boy tightly as Dan gently woke up Nan, who cried at the relief of finally being rescued. She sobbed and sobbed, and she told Jo how sorry she was for getting lost. Jo smiled and told her that no punishment would happen tonight. She was just so pleased to have found them both.

Back at Plumfield, the children were fed a good supper, and everyone fell into a deep sleep after such an active day. The next morning, Nan had a headache and lay on Jo's sofa to rest. Jo gently scolded her for getting lost and roaming away from the group. She even told her stories about her own antics running away and getting lost as a girl. Poor Nan learned her lesson. She felt so terrible for almost losing Rob that in her heart she knew her wild ways must come to an end.

The excitement of Nan and Rob's adventure soon died down, and Plumfield went back to its old routines. Nan's newfound calmness was one cause of welcome peacefulness around the school, but another good influence soon came to stay. Laurie brought his beautiful little daughter, Bess, to visit for an entire week. Everyone loved the little princess and described her as a mix between a fairy and an angel.

Dainty by nature, just having her around the boys calmed them down. Bess didn't like shouting or fighting, and she wouldn't let a single dirty finger touch her, which meant that the boys used a lot of soap that week! Nothing hurt their feelings more than pretty Bess saying, "Go away, dirty boy!"

Despite Nan's recent good behavior, the pretty Bess made her feel a little like a wild bird in a cage. So she tried even harder to be well-behaved. Jo and Father Bhaer laughed about the change in everyone since Bess's arrival.

"The children teach us quite a bit, don't they?" Jo said to her husband one afternoon.

"They certainly do. And I am happy to see Bess bringing out the best in Nan," he replied.

"It's nice to see everyone enjoying themselves, even if it's the calm before the storm," Jo said as she pulled the thread through a button she was sewing onto one of Tommy's shirts.

"What fun they're all having in there." Father Bhaer pointed to the playroom, where Bess was riding on top of a wooden horse. The boys had gathered their chairs around her and were playing Knights of the Round Table.

"Absolutely amazing what the imagination will come up with, isn't it?" Jo said.

Father Bhaer smiled and squeezed his wife's shoulder.

The week with Bess flew by, and before they knew it, Laurie was there to take her home. Parting gifts from all the boys were showered down upon her: white mice, a rabbit, apples, shells, flowers, and minnows were all packed away in the carriage with care. Even Nan, who hated embroidering, had worked her fingers to the bone making a lovely bookmark for the little princess.

As the carriage slowly made its way down the driveway, the children chased after it shouting, "Come back, come back!" until their throats were hoarse and she was out of sight. They all missed Bess in their own way and hoped they would see her again soon.

# CHAPTER 12

# The Storm *after* the Calm

❧

Jo was right about their peaceful week with Bess being the calm before the storm. Two days after she left, a moral earthquake shook Plumfield to its core. As with a fair bit of the trouble that happened with Jo's boys, she found Tommy at its center.

Actually, it was Tommy's hens that were truly at the bottom of the trouble. They were simply laying too many eggs. After he sold all of them and collected a good sum, Father Bhaer insisted he put the money in a piggy bank. As the little bank became heavy with coins, Tommy's imagination filled with all the wonderful things he could buy.

When Jo gave him the four quarters she owed him from the last batch of eggs, Tommy discovered that he was now just one dollar short of the five he'd promised Father Bhaer he would save before breaking open his bank. Tommy raced off to show the shiny money to Nat, who was saving his own money for a new fiddle.

"I wish I had those four quarters to add to my savings," Nat said. "I've only got two dollars toward a new fiddle."

"Maybe I'll lend you some," Tommy said. "I haven't decided yet what I'm going to do with my coins!"

Just then, the boys were interrupted by a voice from outside the barn shouting for them to come and see a jolly great snake that Dan had caught.

Without thinking, Tommy set the money down beside some old farm equipment. The snake was very interesting, and the rest of the day filled up so quickly that Tommy soon forgot to retrieve his quarters from the barn.

*No matter,* he thought before falling asleep, *the only person who knows they are there is Nat.*

The next morning, just as school was getting started, Tommy rushed in to the schoolroom and said, "Who took my dollar?"

"What are you talking about?" Franz asked.

Tommy explained, and Nat seconded his story. At once, everyone declared they knew nothing about it and began to look at Nat suspiciously. The poor boy became more upset and confused each time another boy denied taking the money.

"Well," Franz said, "somebody must have taken it."

Tommy shook his fist in front of everyone and shouted, "Thunder turtles! If I get a hold of the thief . . . he'll be sorry!"

"Keep cool, Tommy," Dan said. "We shall find him out. Thieves always get caught."

The boys all came forward with wild suggestions for what had happened. But Nat could hold his tongue no longer. "I know you think it was me!"

Franz looked at him and said, "You *are* the only one who knew where the money was . . ."

"I can't help that—I didn't take it. I tell you, I didn't take it!" Nat cried.

Father Bhaer heard the commotion and came into the classroom to ask what all the fuss was about. A cloud came over his face when Tommy told him the whole story. He said sternly, "Sit down this instant, all of you."

Then he gave them a very good speech about

the truth and value of honesty and asked each boy just one question: Did they take the money?

Every single boy said no.

When he came to Nat, Father Bhaer's voice softened, for the boy looked so sad. "Now, Nat," he said, "give me an honest answer. Did you take the money?"

Nat said, "No, sir!"

Father Bhaer was very quiet for a moment, and then he said. "I am sorry, Nat, but the evidence is quite against you. We will not punish you until we have proof, but I urge you to tell me the truth. If you are innocent, I will be the first to apologize."

Nat dropped his head onto his arms and sobbed. "I didn't take it. I didn't."

"There is nothing more that can be done now," Father Bhaer said, "and we will not speak of this again. Whoever did take the money will have a hard enough time regaining our trust. Let's get back to our lessons now, shall we?"

The next week was ever so painful for poor Nat. The boys simply refused to talk to him — and for a boy who loved their company, it was the worst thing that could have happened.

Only one person in all of Plumfield believed him, and that was Daisy. She would not hear a bad word spoken against Nat by any of the boys, especially her brother Demi. Even though he was pretty sure Nat had taken the money, Dan stood up for him, too. Still, it made for a very lonely time for the boy.

One afternoon, Dan caught one of the boys bothering Nat by the stream. He broke up the little fight, and once the other boy was gone, Nat said, "That look on your face — I know when you're hiding something. You know who did it! You have to tell, Dan. I can't bear this much longer. If I had anywhere to go, I'd run away, I would."

Dan could not stand to see his dear friend this upset and quickly turned away, muttering, "You won't have to wait for long . . ."

Over the next few days, Dan was moody and short with people, and he didn't participate in any activities. Jo thought showing him how well he'd been doing in the Conscience Book would cheer him up. He looked up at her with a strange expression on his face, a mixture of sadness and pride. "I'm afraid you'll be disappointed in me, but I am trying."

Dan's strange behavior worried Jo, and she felt awful for how hard he was taking Nat's situation.

The next day, Tommy told Nat they could no longer be partners in the egg business. He promptly rubbed out the "& Co." part of his T. Bangs & Co. sign, which truly hurt Nat's feelings.

"I just can't trust you," Tommy said, "no matter how many times you tell me you didn't take the money."

"I can't make you believe me, and I'd give you all of my dollars if you'd only say that you know I didn't do it!" Nat replied.

Tommy just shook his head, "You're on your honor now. You'd better not steal any of my eggs."

Poor Nat was so hurt that he simply could not get over it. He shuffled and moped around the house. One thing made him feel better, and that was the fact that Tommy's hens missed Nat as much as he did them. They hid their eggs so well that they were almost impossible for Tommy to find.

One day, Demi was moving something around in the barn and shouted, "Tommy! Tommy! Come quick, I've found your quarters!"

True enough, the money was there, hidden behind a broken old desk with a note sitting beside it.

"Thunder turtles!" Tommy shouted before

he grabbed them and ran into the house. "Where's Nat! He's given back my money!"

Nat came into the parlor with the rest of the boys. He looked so shocked that they soon realized Nat had nothing to do with putting the money back. The boys examined the note, but no one could tell who wrote it.

"Does it matter," Dan said, "now that the money's back?"

Franz was about to answer the question when Demi burst into the room with a package, "Mrs. Bates next door sent it over—it's addressed to Uncle Bhaer."

Upon hearing his name, Father Bhaer came into the room. He took the package from Demi's outstretched hand and opened up the brown paper.

"Why, that's the book that Uncle Laurie gave to Dan!" Demi said.

As Father Bhaer read the note, he seemed very concerned. "It says here that Dan sold her son Jimmy this book for a dollar last week. She thought it was worth much more than that, so she's sent it back to us. Did you sell it, Dan?"

"Yes, sir."

"Why?" Father Bhaer asked.

Dan answered, "I needed the money."

"What for?"

"To pay someone," Dan replied.

"To pay whom?"

"Tommy." Dan said.

A hush fell over the room. Father Bhaer didn't let any of the boys talk for a moment, but called Jo, who came quickly. "What's happened?" she asked.

Father Bhaer told her the whole story. When he finished, she looked very upset.

Dan said quickly, "I did it. You may do what

you like to me, but I won't say another word about it."

"Not even that you are sorry?" Father Bhaer said.

Dan shook his head. "I'm not sorry."

"We are surprised and disappointed in you," Jo added. "Go up to you room and wait for us there."

The boys were saddened by this turn of events. For the next few days, Father Bhaer and Jo talked at length about what to do. Neither could put their finger on it, but something about Dan's story didn't quite make sense.

Finally, after another torturous week passed, Father Bhaer burst into the classroom one morning shouting, "Dan didn't take the money! We knew he didn't!"

"Who did?" the boys all shouted together.

Father Bhaer pointed to the one empty seat, where a boy named Jack used to sit.

He said, "Jack went home early this morning and left a note saying that he was the one who found the quarters in the barn and was afraid to tell. He was happy to let the blame fall on Nat, but he respected Dan so much that he had to confess. The quarters were in his room."

Father Bhaer handed them back to Tommy, who beamed proudly. Dan stood up and said, "I'd like to say I'm sorry now, for you do understand why I did it—for Nat."

"It was a kind lie," Father Bhaer said, "so of course we all forgive you—although you know now that it's best to be honest, no matter what happens?"

Dan nodded, and the boys cheered.

By now, it was impossible to continue with the lessons, so the little hero and his friends were sent outside to enjoy the rest of the morning. Tommy proudly restored Nat to his partnership, and none were so happy as his poor hens!

CHAPTER 13

# Willow Trees and Energetic Colts!

༂

The old willow tree in the yard at Plumfield was a favorite place for all the children. They climbed up its boughs and left many secrets behind in its leaves. One afternoon after Daisy and Nan finished washing their dolls' clothes in the brook, they decided to perch up in the tree's "nest" until the clothes had all dried.

Their conversation quickly turned from doll clothes to doll furniture and the benefits of feather beds for the dolls' weary heads. For the better part of the afternoon, a long talk about giving up dolls was had, with Daisy worried about how they would fare without their adoptive mother. Nan felt she was simply growing too old to care.

"Oh piddle-paddle. I don't want a house or dolls when I grow up," Nan said. "One day I'll have a room full of bottles and drawers and cure sick people. I'm going to be a doctor—Mother Jo says so."

"Ugh," Daisy said, "How can you stand the bad-smelling stuff and the nasty little powders?"

"Oh, *that* doesn't bother me."

Father Bhaer had shown Nan the herbs in the garden, and she was learning all about them. The boys took to calling her Dr. Giddy-Gaddy, and she adored it. From splinters to stomachaches, Nan cured them all. Jo was ever so pleased at her progress. Nan's "doctoring," as she called it, had helped cure her flighty, tomboy nature.

Daisy looked down and said, "We'd better get

those clothes back up to the house before they blow away."

Down they came from the old willow, and it wasn't but a moment before Nat and Tommy climbed up.

"Now it's safe," Tommy said as he looked around, "and I can tell you a secret."

Nat happily said, "Tell away."

"I've got just the way to make it up to Dan for all of us suspecting him," Tommy answered.

"What's that?"

"I think we should give him a microscope," Tommy replied. "He wants one so terribly, and it would make a jolly good present."

"Tip-top!" Nat cried. "Won't it be expensive, though?"

"Of course it will, but I've got my five dollars, and that should be more than enough," Tommy said.

"What does Father Bhaer think?"

Tommy replied, "He thinks it's a grand idea as well, and I think you should ask if you can come to town with us on Monday to pick it out."

Nat smiled. "And you shall have my three dollars, too. I don't need a new fiddle. My old one suits me just fine. Let's go ask Father Bhaer now if I can come."

Just as Tommy and Nat found their way down from the tree, Demi and Dan returned from a long walk in the woods and climbed up to have a rest in the shade.

They had collected all sorts of leaves on their walk, so naturally Demi wanted to know more about them. The elder boy patiently answered every one of Demi's questions.

When Dan spied Jo and little Teddy coming along underneath them, he said, "Shhh."

Little Teddy cried, "Mama, I want to fish, fish."

But before Jo could break a branch off the tree

to use as a pole, one landed at her feet. She looked up and found Dan and Demi laughing. The minute Teddy saw Dan, he shouted, "Up! Up!"

Demi started down and said, "Yes, Teddy, you can come up because I'm getting down. I've got loads to tell Daisy."

Dan called down to Mother Jo, "Why don't you come up, too—there's lots of room!"

Jo laughed and said, "Well, I haven't been up a tree since I was married. I did use to love to do so when I was a girl. You know, I think I will."

And up she climbed. While Dan made a fishing pole for Teddy, they talked about what a good influence he was becoming on the younger boys. Dan had been working so hard the last few months to be good, and he was very pleased with Jo's words. Their pleasant talk was interrupted by Teddy scrambling down and dropping the fine fishing pole into the brook.

"We'd better watch him," Dan said.

"I think that's a lovely idea—I'll stay up here for a while and read my book."

"You mean I'll be alone?"

Jo laughed. "Why, of course. I trust you, dear boy, and Teddy would have a much better time fishing with you than with me!"

Dan's smile burst from ear to ear. It was the dearest thing to his heart to know that Mother Jo trusted him with her precious son, who felt so much like a brother to him. Teddy and Dan spent a quiet hour by the brook listening to the water rush by, waiting for a fish to bite. Meanwhile, Jo sat, happy as a clam, reading her book. The old willow had never seen or heard so many secrets in one day!

ல

Not long after the lovely afternoon Dan spent with Jo up the old willow tree, she looked out the window to see him racing around the half-mile triangle in the backyard.

"What in the world is that boy doing?" Jo said.

Dan raced around and around the track, pushing himself faster and faster. When he finished, he did somersaults and even tried to jump over the old wall.

"Are you training for a race, Dan?" Jo called out.

He looked up and said, "Just working off some steam!"

"But it's so hot," she shouted. "Be careful you don't make yourself ill."

"I've got to run Mother Jo—I've just got to."

Jo remembered his rough life and knew that it must be hard, after having all that freedom, to stay in one place.

"Is Plumfield too small for you?" she asked. "Do you want to roam?"

Dan kicked the dirt at his feet and said, "I

don't want to, no, but sometimes I feel like I need to get away. That's why I was running out here."

"Well, it's better than fighting, isn't it?"

Dan nodded in agreement.

"Maybe we need to find a way for you to work off your steam around the house and give you a bit of freedom, too. I think you need it," Jo added.

Dan had grown tall and strong and was full of energy. Jo knew that all he needed now was a bit of responsibility.

"I've got it," she said. "How would you like to be my expressman?"

"You mean go into town and do the errands?" Dan asked.

"Exactly! Franz is tired of it, and Father Bhaer doesn't have time. Old Andy's a safe horse, and you are a good driver. Suppose we try it?"

Dan smiled. "I'd like it ever so much, but I'd need to go on my own, without any of the other boys."

Jo thought for a second and then said, "As long as Father Bhaer agrees, it's settled. But you'll have to get up extra early so you can be back in time for school."

Dan grinned. "Oh, I won't mind that—I'm already an early bird."

Father Bhaer did not think it an entirely good idea, but he agreed to a trial period. Dan was up and about early the next morning and made it back in time for school, all of his errands complete. But even the errands weren't enough to use up all of Dan's energy, and soon he was racing around Plumfield again. Father Bhaer led him out into the pasture one afternoon and said, "Here, why don't you wrestle with these trees. The knots and roots all need to be cleared before we can use this field."

Between the errands and the field work, Dan managed to work off a lot of his extra energy. But it wasn't until Laurie's unbroken horse, Charlie, came to Plumfield that he found the perfect way to settle down.

"We understand each other, don't we?" Dan mumbled to Charlie as he nuzzled his head.

Every now and again, Laurie would come to see how Charlie was getting on. He even suggested that the fall would be a good time to try and break him.

Dan said, "He lets me put a halter on him, but I don't think he'll bear a saddle, even if you put it on."

"I shall coax him," Laurie said. "He was mistreated, but I think it will do him good to be broken."

For the next few days, Dan wondered what Charlie would do if he saddled him up. Finally he decided to try it. As soon as the saddle was on Charlie's back and Dan sat down, the horse tossed the boy off. Dan and Charlie played this game with each other for many days. Every time

Dan tried something different to introduce the horse to the saddle, Charlie would outsmart him.

After weeks of trying and lots of bruises, Dan finally broke the colt. When Laurie discovered what the boy had done, he too was pleased, and he gave Dan some riding lessons. Soon, Dan was the only one allowed on Charlie.

❧

Wednesdays were always Essay Day at Plumfield. On one particular Wednesday, all of the children, plus Mother Jo, were out in the museum to listen to the boys present their work. Father Bhaer had finished his final lesson and was about to insist they were done for the day when Tommy shouted, "Wait! We're not done! We must give the *thing*."

"Bless my heart, I forgot! Now is the time, Tommy."

Father Bhaer sat down and Nat, Tommy, and Demi left the room. When they came back, they had a giant red wooden box with them, which they handed to Dan.

"Here you go!" Tommy said. "We wanted to give you something to make up for what happened with my quarters and to show you how happy we are that you came back to Plumfield."

Dan was so surprised, he couldn't speak. He opened up the microscope case and shouted, "What a stunner! It's just what I wanted. Give us a shake, Tommy. It's perfect! Thank you, thank all of you!"

Stepping away from the boys, Dan held his hand out first to Father Bhaer, and then to Mother Jo, and thanked them both. Everyone took a turn looking through the eyepiece at all the wonderful creatures Dan had been collecting all this time for their museum.

Just before closing the museum door and letting the boys have their fun, Jo shouted, "Good job today, my boys. Father Bhaer and I leave you in the capable hands of your new Professor of Natural History!"

On the way back to the main house, Jo and Father Bhaer couldn't help but smile as they thought of how far Dan had come, from taking care of Teddy while fishing to running off his steam in such productive ways.

"I never would have believed it possible," Father Bhaer said, "for that boy to turn out so well."

"Oh, I always knew he had it in him," Jo replied. "I'm just so happy to see him shine now and leave all that nonsense behind him."

# CHAPTER 14

# Thanksgiving and
# the Fun Fall Months

❦

After a successful harvest of all the gardens, Plumfield closed its windows and prepared for fall. With the October frosts came shorter days and longer nights spent by the cheery fire playing games, reading, and talking. But the activity everyone loved the most was storytelling. Each night Mother Jo or Father Bhaer would tell the boys a tall tale. Sometimes they would be so scared by the end of the story that heading upstairs for the night became an adventure of looking under beds and opening up closet doors.

One night, when everyone was getting up to mischief and calling one another names in the playroom, Franz, who was watching them, decided that enough was enough.

"From now on, everyone who enters the room must tell a story—those are the rules. And no more jokes, especially you, Tommy. It will be fun to see who comes in first."

Tommy scowled at being the only one called out and said, "Thunder turtles!" under his breath.

The boys didn't have long to wait before Mother Jo came into the room to find Nan. She was making a new dress for the growing girl and needed to measure her. The boys led Jo into the playroom by the hand and demanded a story. She laughed and said, "Am I the first meek mouse you cats have caught?"

"Yes!" Tommy shouted. "But who better to start off our game with than you, Mother Jo?"

"Well, what shall I tell you about?" Jo wondered. "I know. I'll tell you the tale of 'The Suspected Boy.'"

Before she started, she smiled and winked at Nat, who blushed a little, as he always did when someone paid attention to him. Then Jo told a story about a small boy living in a house, somewhat like Plumfield, filled up with boys who needed to be taught lessons like not stealing gooseberries and always telling the truth.

Jo was about to start her second story when little Rob came tumbling into the playroom in his pajamas. "I heard noise," he said as he rubbed his eyes, "and I wanted to know what was going on."

"You march right back into bed," Jo said, but she was interrupted by Demi, who shouted, "He has to tell us a story, Aunt Jo. It's the law!"

Rob's story was three lines long and involved a water pump, a boy, and a great fall—much to the merriment of all listening.

Then Father Bhaer came into the room saying, "What's going on in here?"

The children all fell into laughter once again and enforced their law. Father Bhaer sat down beside his wife and put his hand on his chin for a moment. "I know the perfect story!" he said.

Eyes grew wide and there were shouts of "oh no!" and "really!" as Father Bhaer told the tale of the time Jo's father, known to them as Grandfather March, was almost robbed—and how his kindness toward the man stopped the evil deed from happening. At the end of the story, Father Bhaer stood up. The boys surrounded him, trying to pull him back down to tell another story. He barely escaped to his study, and he sent the laughing boys racing back into the playroom.

Finally the boys settled on a lively game of blind man's bluff, and apologies were made for earlier name calling. By the time the night bell rang for bed, imaginations were stirring from a grand night of storytelling.

∽

As the fall progressed, everyone grew more and more excited. Thanksgiving was by far the favorite holiday at Plumfield. For days beforehand, the girls helped Jo and Asia in the kitchen, making pies and puddings, dusting off the good dishes, and sorting fruit. The boys hovered outside, impatient to taste whatever was cooking—it smelled so delicious! A general air of hustle and bustle filled the house. Even the great pumpkin Rob had grown in the garden couldn't help but be busy— it was turned into a half-dozen golden pies!

When at last the day came, the boys went off for a long walk in the woods so they might have a grand appetite for dinner. The girls stayed back and helped set the table before they hid themselves away in the schoolroom to prepare a grand performance. Hardy little Teddy stood guard at the schoolroom door and refused to let anyone in, especially his father.

When Nan finally came out of the room, she said, "It's all done, and it's perfect!"

Daisy added, "Franz knows exactly what to do now, and then we're all set."

"The boys are coming," Nan said. "I hear them now. We'd better go get ready for dinner."

The girls raced upstairs to get dressed in their good clothes as the boys returned from their walk. Faces were scrubbed and jackets were brushed off and put on. With combed hair and glowing cheeks, the children filed into the dining room the minute the bell rang.

The meal contained so many wonderful things the children had grown themselves that they each went around the table pointing out what their hard work had brought to the table.

When everyone had finished, Rob asked, "But who made Thanksgiving?"

Father Bhaer said, "I know many boys who can answer that question."

He nodded to Demi who said, "The Pilgrims made it."

"What for?" Rob asked.

Demi rubbed his forehead and thought for a minute before admitting that he just didn't remember.

"I think Demi meant to remember that the Pilgrims had one terrible harvest and swore always for be thankful for a good one," Dan added.

Father Bhaer turned to Rob and said, "Do you understand?"

"Not really," Rob answered. "I thought Pilgrims were a sort of big bird that lived on rocks. I saw pictures in Demi's book."

Jo laughed. "My word, he means penguins!"

The whole table burst into laughter at the thought of the penguins sitting down for a delicious Thanksgiving meal.

By now, Demi had remembered the whole story and said, "If I may, Aunt Jo, I'd like to tell it."

Jo nodded, and Demi stood up so everyone could hear. He told a splendid story about the Pilgrims and the very first Thanksgiving, and everyone clapped once it was finished.

After dinner, Father Bhaer took everyone for a drive, leaving Jo behind to finish up the final details of the girls' performance. The whole family was expected: Grandfather and Grandmother March, Demi and Daisy's father and mother, and Laurie and his lovely wife, Jo's sister Amy. By the time the children got back from the drive, everyone was there.

"Come into the schoolroom for the show!" Jo called out, and the whole merry flock came in and took their seats. A grand play starring Bess as the little princess was acted out, complete with stage tricks and brilliant costumes. The girls had worked on it all day and even made Laurie drop Bess of early so they could practice. The curtain had barely fallen before applause rang out in the little room.

At last, Nat came out with his fiddle and played a song that Uncle Laurie had written for Jo, which brought tears to her eyes. Nat tried to leave the stage again and again, but was brought back three different times for encores. He would have done more if Tommy had not insisted that they clear the chairs so everyone could dance.

Laurie came to stand beside Jo as she watched the boys twirl the girls, having practiced at length to get the steps just right.

"What are you thinking about here in the corner of the room?" he asked.

Jo smiled at her old friend. "Just imagining the future of my boys."

Laurie said, "They'll be poets, painters, statesmen, and famous soldiers—or at least good businessmen."

"Well, I would be happy if they all turned out to be good men," she said.

As Jo looked around the room at each of her boys, recognizing their special talents and all the ways they had changed in such a short time, she said, "They have all worked so hard, though none as hard as Nat and Dan."

"What magic did you use, Jo?"

"None but love on my part," she answered. "But they had a good teacher." She nodded her head in the direction of Father Bhaer, happily twirling little Teddy around the room to the music.

Jo and Laurie were soon joined by Father Bhaer and the rest of the family, who stood together, watching the children enjoying themselves after a long year of hard work. Jo looked around the room at every one of her boys, her heart as full as one can be with love, and smiled. She was happy and content, and she knew that her little school at Plumfield would always be a success.

# What Do *You* Think?
## Questions for Discussion

⌒᷐

Have you ever been around a toddler who keeps asking the question "Why?" all the time? Does your teacher call on you in class with questions from your homework? Do your parents ask you questions about your day at the dinner table? We are always surrounded by questions that need a specific response. But is it possible to have a question with no right answer?

The following questions are about the book you just read. But this is not a quiz! They are designed to help you look at the people, places, and events in the story from different angles. These questions do not have specific answers. Instead, they might make you think of the story in a completely new way.

Think carefully about each question and enjoy discovering more about this classic story.

1. When Nat first arrives at Plumfield, he sees the boys entertaining themselves in a number of ways. Which seemed the most exciting to you? What do you like to do on rainy days?

2. Where does Demi say is the nicest place in the world? Why does he think this? Where do you think is the nicest place?

3. Why do Jo and Father Bhaer allow the boys a weekly pillow fight? Do you have any bedtime rituals?

4. How do Jo's boys make money? What do you do to earn extra spending money?

5. Mother Jo says she would like to grow some patience in her magical garden. What do the boys say they would grow? What would you grow in your magical garden?

6. How does Daisy react when Jo reveals the toy kitchen she built for her? Did you guess what the surprise was? What is your favorite toy anyone ever gave you?

7. Laurie suggests that the boys build a museum to show off their most prized possessions. Who is in charge of the museum? What would you add to such a museum?

8. Why does Dan say that he took Tommy's money? Have you ever lied to protect a friend?

9. Where do Jo's boys go when they want privacy? Where do you go when you want to be alone?

10. Nan says that she would like to be a doctor when she grows up. What would you like to be?

# Afterword
*By Arthur Pober, Ed.D.*

❧

First impressions are important.

Whether we are meeting new people, going to new places, or picking up a book unknown to us, first impressions count for a lot. They can lead to warm, lasting memories or can make us shy away from any future encounters.

Can you recall your own first impressions and earliest memories of reading the classics?

Do you remember wading through pages and pages of text to prepare for an exam? Or were you the child who hid under the blanket to read with a flashlight, joining forces with Robin Hood to save Maid Marian? Do you remember only how long it took you to read a lengthy novel such as *Little Women*? Or did you become best friends with the March sisters?

Even for a gifted young reader, getting through long chapters with dense language can easily become overwhelming and can obscure the richness of the story and its characters. Reading an abridged, newly crafted version of a classic novel can be the gentle introduction a child needs to explore the characters and storyline without the frustration of difficult vocabulary and complex themes.

Reading an abridged version of a classic novel gives the young reader a sense of independence and the satisfaction of finishing a "grown-up" book. And when a child is engaged with and inspired by a classic story, the tone is set for further exploration of the story's themes, characters, history, and details. As a child's reading skills advance, the desire to tackle the original, unabridged version of the story will naturally emerge.

If made accessible to young readers, these stories can become invaluable tools for understanding themselves in the context of their families and social environments. This is why the Classic Starts series includes questions that stimulate discussion regarding the impact and social relevance of the characters and stories today. These questions can foster lively conversations between children and their parents or teachers. When we look at the issues, values, and standards of past times in terms of how we live now, we can appreciate literature's classic tales in a very personal and engaging way.

Share your love of reading the classics with a young child, and introduce an imaginary world real enough to last a lifetime.

## Dr. Arthur Pober, Ed.D.

Dr. Arthur Pober has spent more than twenty years in the fields of early childhood and gifted education. He is the former principal of one of the world's oldest laboratory schools for gifted youngsters, Hunter College Elementary School, and former Director of Magnet Schools for the Gifted and Talented for more than 25,000 youngsters in New York City.

Dr. Pober is a recognized authority in the areas of media and child protection and is currently the U.S. representative to the European Institute for the Media and European Advertising Standards Alliance.

Explore these wonderful stories in our
Classic Starts™ library.

*The Red Badge of Courage*

*Robinson Crusoe*

*The Secret Garden*

*The Story of King Arthur and His Knights*

*The Strange Case of Dr. Jekyll and Mr. Hyde*

*The Swiss Family Robinson*

*The Three Musketeers*

*The Time Machine*

*Treasure Island*

*The Voyages of Doctor Dolittle*

*The War of the Worlds*

*White Fang*

*The Wind in the Willows*